Alan Gibbons

THE LION ROARS

With illustrations by
Chris Chalik

*To the Char Char Trust and
Ndi Moyo Clinic, Malawi*

First published in 2016 in Great Britain by
Barrington Stoke Ltd
18 Walker Street, Edinburgh, EH3 7LP

www.barringtonstoke.co.uk

Text © 2016 Alan Gibbons
Illustrations © 2016 Chris Chalik

The moral right of Alan Gibbons and Chris Chalik to be
identified as the author and illustrator of this work has
been asserted in accordance with the Copyright, Designs
and Patents Act, 1988

A CIP catalogue record for this book is available
from the British Library upon request

ISBN: 978-1-78112-563-2

Printed in China by Leo

Contents

Chapter One
The Cub

For most of the boys Jimi knew, it was books or football, but Jimi loved books *and* football.

Of course, most of the books he read were about football. Jimi's mum and dad were always telling him to read.

"Books give you an education," they said. "You can make something of yourself, be a lawyer, a doctor, a teacher. Or you could have your own shop or factory."

'Just think,' Jimi dreamed, 'one day I might drive up to my house with my mum and dad, my brother and sister, and walk inside like somebody important in my well-cut suit.'

But Jimi knew that football gives you an even bigger dream. Football can make you into a star. A star so big that people will read about you in the newspapers and see you on TV.

And so Jimi played football every spare minute he had. He played after school. Sometimes he went down to the beach with his friends and they used the palm trees as goal posts. They all played in their bare feet – they only had one pair of shoes each, and they had to keep those smart. Then they would race through the waves and splash each other. Jimi played everywhere, every place and every time he could. He would have played in his sleep if he could. He played with joy in his heart and magic in his toes.

Jimi played with pride, too. He was proud to be African.

In Jimi's school there were books about all the great footballers born in Africa. He knew their names off by heart – Roger Milla and Patrick Vieira, Samuel Eto'o and Patrice Evra, Demba Ba and Didier Drogba. There was music in their names and in the names of the great African national teams – the Elephants, the Panthers, the Eagles, the Lions.

Jimi wanted to wear the all-white kit of the Lions of Senegal one day. Every day he imagined himself running out onto the pitch in front of thousands of fans, hearing them chant his name. "Jimi, Jimi Diop." It was a wonderful dream, but Jimi couldn't think how it might come true.

Today Jimi was playing with his friend Demba.

"Hey Jimi," Demba shouted. "You might be our star player, but you need to cut out the daydreams!"

Jimi jogged over to join in. Demba was right – he was their star player. All the boys his own age wanted him in their team. With Jimi on side they would win for sure. But he was always looking over at the older boys, like his brother Nuru. They would never let Jimi play with them.

When the game ended, Jimi went over to stand by his sister Julia, who was watching Nuru play. They always waited for Nuru so the three of them could walk home together.

"Did you win?" Julia asked Jimi.

"I won," Jimi said. "I scored four goals. I always win. I'm too good for the boys my age."

Nuru came over to take a throw-in.

"Hey, when are you going to let me play on your team?" Jimi asked.

"You?" one of Nuru's friends said. "You belong with the little kids."

"Come back when you've grown a bit," another one added.

"Yes, go and play with the other runts."

"Who are you calling a runt?" Jimi asked. "I'm no runt. I'm a lion. I can play better than any of you."

That made them all laugh.

"You are not a lion," they teased. "You are just a cub – and the smallest cub at that. Go back to the babies. Runt."

Their laughter and jeers made Jimi's neck hot with anger. He was better than all the little kids put together and he had more skill than any of the older boys, even Nuru. He would show them if only they would give him a chance.

Julia bent forward and whispered in his ear. "You come with me," she said.

"But I want to play with them," Jimi protested.

"You will," Julia said. "Soon. You need to practise first."

Jimi pulled a face.

"Don't do that," Julia said. "It will stick and you'll look like a grumpy little boy all your life."

Demba was still around, so they played attack and defence with Demba in goal and Julia in defence. Jimi was in attack.

Julia was a great defender. She was older than the boys and tall and strong, and she kept pushing Jimi off the ball. The second time she knocked him over, he sat in the dust, crossed his arms and sulked with that grumpy look on his face again.

"That's not fair," he moaned. "You're not playing football. You just keep shoving me."

"If it's so easy for me to push you off the ball," Julia said, "just think what Nuru and his friends will do. You have to be strong."

Jimi jumped up. "I am strong," he said. "I'm as strong as a lion!"

"You have to be strong here and here," Julia told him, and she slapped his arms and legs. "You need some proper muscles, my mighty lion cub." Then she tapped his head. "You have to be strong here too."

Jimi frowned.

"Do you mean I have to head the ball? Easy. I can do that." He looked at Demba. "Tell her."

"He's right," Demba said. "He scores lots of goals with his head."

Julia laughed. "I don't just mean heading the ball," she said. "I mean *thinking*. In football, the first step is in your head. If you can think faster than your opponent, you can beat him, even when he is bigger than you."

Julia played football herself. She was captain of her team and knew what she was talking about. Jimi would be a fool not to listen to her.

"Do you want me to show you?" she asked.

Jimi looked at Demba. Demba shrugged.

"You never know," he said. "Your sister is good."

"OK," Julia said. "Rule number 1. Don't lose your temper. Rule number 2. Don't sulk. Rule number 3. Think. Think faster than the

defender. When you see him coming, you need a plan."

Three times more, Julia knocked Jimi off the ball. The next time she came to tackle him, he ran for the ball and made up a plan in his head. He skipped over her leg, pushed the ball out to her left and scored. It was Julia's turn to sit in the dust.

"That's my little brother," Julia said, getting to her feet and ruffling his hair.

Jimi smiled.

"Wait till I get a game with the older boys," he said. "I'll show them."

"But remember," Julia said. "Have the brains of a teacher and the roar of a lion."

HOW AFRICAN FOOTBALL BEGAN

Football is the most popular sport in Africa.

It came to Africa over a hundred years ago with Europeans when they had colonies in Africa. Over the years, many teams and leagues were set up.

Egypt was the first African team to appear in the FIFA World Cup in 1934.

The Confederation of African Football was set up in 1957.

Zaire played well in the World Cup in 1974 and gave Scotland a scare, but they didn't win. The first African team to win a World Cup match was Tunisia in 1978. They came back from 0–1 down to win 3–1.

Now, in the 21st century, African teams are a major force in world football. African teams such as Cameroon, Senegal and Ivory Coast often reach the later stages of the World Cup and players from Africa are some of the top stars in the best clubs across the world.

Chapter Two
Paws of Gold

Jimi stopped sulking and he stopped losing his temper, but he never stopped asking the older boys if he could play with them.

"No, you play with the little kids, Cub," one said.

"Yes, stick with the runts," another told him.

"Play with the big boys and you'll get hurt," Nuru said.

That hurt most of all. Jimi looked up to Nuru, but Nuru didn't want Jimi to make him look stupid in front of his friends. He didn't want Jimi hanging round with them.

"You read your books," Nuru said. "You'll be a professor some day."

One evening Jimi was sitting on the step outside his house, looking down the street. Julia came and sat next to him.

"What are you thinking about, little brother?" she asked.

"I'm working on a plan," Jimi said.

That night, Jimi crawled under his bed and pulled out a roll of paper with an elastic band round it. This was his prized map of the world. Jimi's dad brought it back for him when he went to work in Dakar, the capital of Senegal. When Jimi read about the great football leagues in South America and Europe, he picked them out on his map. Brazil, Argentina, Spain, Italy, France, Germany, England ...

'Dreams are like clouds,' Jimi thought. 'They are real, but you can't touch them.' But he could touch his map. And he could draw the flags of all the different countries. Brazil was green, yellow and blue. Argentina was blue and white. Germany was red, black and gold. England's flag was red and white and the flag of France was red, white and blue.

When he was done with the flags, he used to draw little football shirts and add the colours of the best teams in the world – Barcelona, Real Madrid, Bayern Munich, Juventus, Manchester United and Paris Saint-Germain. He laid out the flags and shirts and imagined playing for Senegal against England, or for Barcelona against Paris Saint-Germain.

The next day, Jimi's uncle Dani came over. Like Jimi and Julia, Dani lived for football. He was the best defender in his local side and Jimi's dad said French scouts had watched Dani a few times.

That morning, Dani bent down next to Jimi and looked at the map.

"Will I ever get to play for one of those teams?" Jimi asked.

"You've got the talent and the energy," Dani said. "And you've got a big heart, but lots of kids dream of making it in France or Spain or England. You need plenty of luck too."

"Dad says you've got luck," Jimi told his uncle. "Haven't the scouts been watching you?"

"Yes." Uncle Dani nodded. "They've been to the club twice. They've asked me to go with them to Paris."

"That's where Paris Saint-Germain play," Jimi said.

Dani put his arm round Jimi, "If I make it," he said, "I'll help your parents save up the money to fly you out to France. You can live with me and show the local teams what you can do. Would you like that?"

"Too right I would!" Jimi cried. "Paris! Me? Do you mean it?"

"Yes," Dani said with a smile.

But then a cloud passed over Jimi's face. "What about mum and dad?" he said. "What about Julia?" He thought for a moment. "And Nuru?"

"The plane fare costs a fortune," Dani said. "I'd love you all to come, but none of us can afford it."

Jimi knew his uncle was right, but his words made him sad. Maybe he would stay. How could he leave his family?

*

The next day after school, Jimi and Julia were watching Nuru play. One of the boys on his team went down hard. He gripped his leg in pain.

"That's it," Nuru said. "He can't play now. You take his place, Julia. You're better than half the boys here."

He was right. They had just set up a girls' team, and Julia had been everyone's first choice as their captain.

"OK," Julia said, "I will play, but then you let Jimi play the last ten minutes."

"You're crazy," one of the boys said. "The cub can't play. Somebody will tread on him."

"Yes," another boy said. "We'll squash him flat."

At that, Jimi lost his temper. "I'll squash you," he growled.

"You stand here and watch," Julia said, and she gave Jimi her hard look. "I'll give you your chance."

Julia was true to her word. She played for ten minutes, then she swapped places with Jimi. The other boys shook their heads as Jimi ran onto the pitch. It was 3–3 and, to begin with, Jimi couldn't get the ball. Nobody passed to him.

Then, all of a sudden, the ball ran free and he pounced on it.

"Go, Cub, go!" Julia shouted.

Jimi danced past the defence in his bare feet. He beat two boys and nutmegged the third. He skipped round a tackle and slid the ball under the keeper's body.

"Goal!"

Jimi ran over to Julia and high-fived her.

Julia grinned. "I said you would get your chance," she said.

After that, Jimi was on fire. He set up one goal and scored another. His team won 6–3. Nuru lifted Jimi up on his shoulders, grabbed Jimi's bare feet and waggled them in front of all the boys.

"Did you see my little brother?" he boasted. "Did you see what he did?"

"I saw it," another boy said. He was the one who had called Jimi a runt. "I just don't believe it."

"You better believe it," Nuru said. "The cub has paws of gold."

WHEN THE THREE LIONS GOT A FRIGHT

It is the 1st of July, 1990.

It is hot in the San Paolo Stadium in Naples, Italy.

Few of the 55,000 fans watching expect this quarter-final to turn into an epic battle. They are sure that England – winners of the World Cup in 1966 – will beat their African opponents, Cameroon. When England take the lead with a David Platt header, some say it looks to be all over.

But then, after 61 minutes, 38-year-old Roger Milla comes on and changes the game as he sets up the pass that leads to a penalty.

1–1.

Milla then sets up Eugène Ekéké.

2–1.

Cameroon are in dream land. Milla is involved again. He plays a one-two with François Omam-Biyik. Omam-Biyik must score ... but he doesn't. There are seven minutes to go. Can Cameroon hang on to their lead?

Then disaster. England go down in the box at the other end and win a penalty. Gary Lineker scores.

2–2.

It is extra time.

And then – oh no, another penalty. Lineker again.

2–3.

It is all over. England have won – just.

Cameroon have lived up to their nickname, the Indomitable Lions. In their green shirts and red shorts, they do a lap of honour at the end of one of the great matches of the 1990 World Cup.

Chapter Three
The Lion's First Steps

Jimi always played with the big boys after he won the 6–3 match for them.

When they tried to bully him with their strength, he was able to skip out of the way. When they tried to tackle him, he used his skill to avoid their challenges. He liked to twist and turn, sprint and dribble. He could do step overs and pull the ball back to wrong-foot his marker.

As he got faster and stronger, Jimi started to play with a local club. Nuru was captain and he would always look out for his little brother when the other players got a bit rough.

Jimi, Nuru and Julia all loved it when Uncle Dani came to watch. They would miss him when he left for France. Mum and Dad were proud that their children were stars of their teams, but they also thought school was more important than football. With Uncle Dani, it was the other way round. He reminded them to do their stretches before and after each game. He hugged them when they did something well. He showed them new tricks. They played better when he was there on the touchline to support them. After each match, he walked home with them. He always said the same thing to Jimi before he left.

"Keep practising, Cub. You need talent to make it, but you'll get nowhere without hard work."

One day, Uncle Dani had big news. The scout had been to see him and needed him to leave for France very soon.

"But when?" Jimi asked. "It is our tournament next week. You are coming to see me, aren't you?"

"I will do my very best, Cub," Uncle Dani said, "but as soon as my papers are sorted, I have to go."

"Papers?" Jimi said. "What papers?"

"Forms, Cub," Uncle Dani said. "We need to fill in lots of forms so they will let me into France."

Uncle Dani was there for the quarter-final, when Jimi got a penalty. Nuru scored from the spot and put the team through to the semi-final. Jimi heard people talking about him as he left the pitch at full-time. He thought his heart was going to burst out of his chest with pride.

"Did you see that little kid?" one man said. "He ran the show. He's special."

Uncle Dani was there for the semi-final too. This was the hardest game Jimi had ever played in. He couldn't get into the match. The defenders had heard all about him and two of them blocked everything he tried to do. They were 2–0 down at half-time. The coach turned to Uncle Dani.

"Is there anything you want to say?" he asked.

Uncle Dani thought for a moment.

"Why don't you play Nuru behind Jimi up front?" he said. "Nuru can protect Cub from the defenders."

The coach said he would try the tactic. It worked. Nuru acted as a shield. The defenders bounced off him. Jimi scored one goal and set up a second. It was 2–2.

"Go, Cub, go," Uncle Dani yelled. Jimi's mum and dad were standing next to him.

The ball ran free and Nuru pounced on it, turned and rolled it into the penalty area. Jimi ran onto it and side-footed it home. 2–3. They were in the final!

"You were a monster out there," Dad said.

Jimi knew what Mum was going to tell him.

"Just don't forget your studies," she said. "Football is a dream. Education is what you need in life."

Three days later it was the final. As they walked out onto the pitch, Jimi and Nuru looked for Uncle Dani.

"Where is he?" Jimi asked as they kicked off. He felt glum that Uncle Dani wasn't there to watch them.

The game was even harder than the semi-final. Jimi was having an off day. And Nuru's heart wasn't in it either. They were lucky to be only 2–1 down at half-time. That's when they saw Dad.

They ran over to him. "Where's Uncle Dani?" they asked.

"Sorry, boys," Dad said. "I've just been to the airport with him. His papers got sorted and he had to fly out this morning."

Jimi and Nuru couldn't believe that their uncle had left without saying goodbye. They tried to be pleased for him and to play better in the second half, but things just didn't feel the same without Uncle Dani to cheer them on.

They lost 5–1.

TWO AFRICAN GREATS

There have been many great African footballers. Here are two of them.

Samuel Eto'o of Cameroon is the most decorated African player of all time. He has won African Player of the Year four times – a record. He was third in FIFA World Player of the Year in 2005.

In 2010, Eto'o became the first player to win two European trebles, with Inter Milan and Barcelona. He scored over 100 goals in five seasons with Barcelona.

He was a winner of La Liga (Spain) three times and Serie A (Italy) once.

He was a winner of the Copa Del Rey (Spain) twice and the Coppa Italia (Italy) twice.

He was a Champions League winner three times.

He was a winner of both the World Cup and the European Championships with France.

At the start of the 2015/16 season Samuel Eto'o made his debut for the Turkish side Antalyaspor.

Patrick Vieira was born in Senegal, but his family moved to France when he was 8. He played international football for France. He was Captain for three years and won 107 caps. Vieira was part of the squad that won the 1998 World Cup and he and his team-mates were made Knights of the Légion d'honneur. In 2001, Vieira was French Player of the Year.

Vieira was a Premier League winner three times and an FA Cup winner four times with Arsenal.

He was also an FA Cup winner with Manchester City.

He was a Serie A (Italy) winner three times with Inter Milan and once with Juventus.

Patrick Vieira retired from professional football in 2011.

Chapter Four
The Cub Leaves Home

Jimi and Nuru tried to pick themselves up and dust themselves down after the defeat in the final. They needed to make Uncle Dani proud of them, just like they were so proud of him.

Before long, Dani was a real professional – a player in his club's first team in the French second division.

Jimi pinned the photos and programmes Dani sent home all over the wall of the bedroom he shared with Nuru. He took out his map, found the town where Dani was playing and coloured in a football shirt to stick on it.

But he still felt like his uncle was a long way away. One day Jimi was sitting on the beach with a book about France in his hands. Julia found him staring out at the waves, watching the sun play on the water.

"Mum sent me to find you," Julia said. "Are you all right?"

"Yes, I'm fine," Jimi said. "I just miss Uncle Dani. Mum and Dad don't get football the way he does."

Julia sat down next to him. "But I do."

Jimi knew Julia was right – she loved football more than anything, just like him. He sighed. "It's just ... when Uncle Dani was here, my dream of playing for a big team didn't seem that far away. He made it seem real. Now he's gone, I don't think it will ever happen."

"Cheer up, Cub," Julia said. "*You* can make your dreams come true, you know."

Jimi gazed out at the sea. 'Maybe for other people,' he thought. 'Not for me.' He remembered how they lost the final. That still hurt.

Weeks went by. Months passed. Jimi worked hard in school, played football, grew taller and stronger. He helped his team win the local league. Nuru was the captain, but Jimi was the star player. One day, a week after their team won the league, Jimi walked in the door to find a visitor in the house. Uncle Dani!

"You didn't say you were coming," he yelled with excitement. Uncle Dani had presents for them all – a pair of brand new football boots each for Jimi, Julia and Nuru.

"The season has finished in France," Dani explained. "I'm back until we start training for the new season."

Then Dani looked across at Mum and Dad. "Do we tell him?"

Jimi frowned. He could see that Julia and Nuru were in on the secret too. "Tell me what?" he asked. "Is something wrong?"

"Are you joking, little brother?" Nuru said. "You're going to be a big star."

"That's right," Julia said. "You're going to France."

Jimi couldn't believe his own ears. "For a holiday?" he asked.

"No," Dad said. "To live. Your uncle Dani has told his manager about you. He's interested. If you keep going like you are, you'll get a trial."

Jimi punched the air.

"France. I'm going to France." He looked around, eyes shining. "Are we all going?"

"No," Mum said. "We can only afford for you to go."

The joy died in Jimi's eyes as fast as it had appeared. "But you're my family."

Dad put his hands on Jimi's shoulders.

"You will live with Uncle Dani," he said. "He has a nice room for you in his flat. You will come home during the holidays. You will go to school and play your football. We all know it is your dream."

*

That is how Jimi came to live with Uncle Dani in France. He held back the tears when he said goodbye to his family at the airport. He didn't let them come until Uncle Dani fell asleep on the plane. Jimi was a lion and lions don't cry.

Soon, Jimi got used to life in France. He made friends at his new school. Dani's club were impressed and signed him as a junior. After school, he would sit in his room and look at his map, dreaming of playing in La Liga, the Bundesliga, Serie A, the Premiership.

One day, Uncle Dani came to see how Jimi was doing in training.

"What do you think?" he asked the coach. "Back home he was always too small. The other boys used to push him off the ball."

"Just look at him," the coach said. "Being pushed off the ball's not the problem."

Uncle Dani frowned. "So what is the problem?"

"Watch."

Uncle Dani saw what the coach meant. Jimi was hogging the ball, trying to do everything himself. He would try to beat three players on his own and end up losing the ball.

"I've told him this isn't the way to prove himself," the coach said. "But it's in one ear and out the other." He sighed. "Can you talk to him?"

"I'll try."

But Jimi didn't want to listen to his uncle either.

"The other boys are jealous of me," he said.

"Don't say that in front of them," Uncle Dani said. "They'll think you're big-headed. You have to play for the team."

Jimi scowled and went to his room to sulk and to brood on the trial that was coming up. If he did well, he'd get into the youth team. If he didn't, the club might let him go.

On the day of the trial, Jimi played his heart out. He rushed forward in attack, raced back to defend. He was everywhere and couldn't understand why he was on the losing side.

"Ten minute break," the coach said as he blew his whistle.

"How's it going?" Uncle Dani asked Jimi.

"I don't know," Jimi said. "Nobody will pass to me."

"Are you passing to them?" Uncle Dani asked.

"No, but ..." Jimi said. "I have to get the ball myself. I am working my heart out, but the other team is winning.

"That's because you're only playing with your heart," Uncle Dani said. "Use your brain. You can't do everything yourself. You'll just wear yourself out and lose the ball."

Jimi nodded, then went and sat alone. He remembered that Julia had said something like that back home in Senegal.

The coach blew his whistle for the end of the break and Jimi was determined to play a different game this half. He didn't try to do everything himself, but started passing the ball instead. Soon, his team was in control.

Jimi got the ball on the left. He held it, then saw his team-mate, Patrice, race into the box. He passed the ball – a perfect cross – and Patrice scored.

The score was level now. The game looked like it was heading for a draw when Patrice got the ball. This time Jimi made the run, Patrice rolled the ball in front of him and Jimi lobbed the keeper.

"Goal!"

As Jimi's team celebrated, Uncle Dani glanced at the coach.

"I see you had a word with young Jimi," he said, and a broad smile lit up his face.

Uncle Dani nodded, and he was smiling too. "So he did enough?" he asked. "Will you play him in the youth team?"

"He did enough." The coach shook Uncle Dani's hand. "I have great hopes for Jimi."

DIDIER DROGBA – A LEGEND IN BLUE

Didier Drogba is from the Ivory Coast and he is the all-time top scorer for the Ivory Coast national team with 65 goals in 104 appearances.

After playing as a professional in France, Didier Drogba made his debut for Chelsea in 2004, and in 2012, fans voted him Chelsea's greatest ever player. With Chelsea he won the Premier League four times, the FA Cup three times and the League Cup three times, and scored more goals for the club than any other foreign player. He played his last game for Chelsea in May 2015.

Drogba has also won the Champions League, and he won the league and the Turkish Super Cup when he played for Galatasary in Turkey.

Didier Drogba has won the African Footballer of the Year award twice, in 2006 and 2009. In August 2015, the fans of Montreal Impact of Canada went wild when Drogba kicked off the new season with them!

Chapter Five
The Lion Has Claws

Uncle Dani switched off the TV and sat next to Jimi in the living room.

"The coach says you can make it, Jimi," he said. "You're fast and skilful and you're starting to play with your head as well as your heart."

Jimi liked what he heard, but he knew what everybody said about him.

"I'm still a bit small," he said, "and I'm not strong enough on the ball."

"You'll get there," Uncle Dani said. "You just have to work on building your strength. You need to put in some extra hours. Are you ready to do that?"

Jimi nodded. "When do I start?"

"Right now," Uncle Dani said.

Uncle Dani and Jimi drove to the park. Dani opened the boot of the car.

"Meet Mr Tyre and Mr Rope," he said.

Jimi stared. "What are they for?" he asked.

"I'll show you." Uncle Dani laughed.

Uncle Dani tied the rope round the tractor tyre and soon Jimi was dragging it across the park, then flipping it over and over again.

After that it was press-ups, chin-ups, squat jumps, star jumps, tuck jumps and burpees. After Uncle Dani's routine, Jimi didn't stop to rest. He came up with some ideas of his own, inspired by the kids he'd seen doing parkour and free running. And, from then on, he stopped walking to school and started running all the way, leaping off steps and vaulting over barriers.

"Fast as a lion," he told himself as he ran. "Strong as a lion."

At the next training session, the coach had some news for the squad. They were going to play in an international tournament.

"There will be teams from England, Germany, Spain and Italy," the coach said. "Scouts will come along to look for new talent. This could be your big chance, boys."

He called each player over to discuss his strengths and weaknesses. "What do you think I'm going to say to you, Jimi?" the coach asked.

"Be strong," Jimi said. "Play for the team."

The coach winked. "You have a good football brain. Use it."

Jimi stared at him. "Is that it?"

"That's it."

And so Jimi played deeper, using his passing skills to put his team-mates in on goal. He used his brain to lead his team to the final, where their opponents were an English side. Uncle Dani slapped Jimi on the back as he led the team out.

"A lion against the three lions," he said. "Good luck."

The coach had something to say too. "They're a big side, Jimi. Tough and very physical. They know you run things, so they'll come after you."

Jimi remembered all the hours he'd spent dragging that tyre across the park. It was time to see if it had worked.

The coach was right. Every time he got the ball, two English players followed him. They tugged his shirt, tackled him and pushed him off the ball. For most of the first half, he found it hard to get into the game.

At half-time it was 1–1.

"There's a scout here," Uncle Dani told him during the break. He pointed the man out to Jimi. "He's come to watch you," he said, "but it looks like he won't stay for much longer. It's now or never. You need to up your game."

"Now or never," Jimi repeated to himself as he went out for the second half. He felt like a different player. When his markers tackled, he dug in and battled his way past. When they shoved him, he shoved back. He stood firm.

With ten minutes to go it was 2–2. Jimi lost one of his markers. The second crashed an elbow into Jimi's ribs. Jimi winced, but he rode the challenge, nutmegged his man and smashed

the ball into the net. As he turned away from the goal he saw his marker sitting on his backside. Jimi grinned and jogged past him.

Uncle Dani gave him the thumbs-up, then raised both hands. "They tried to bully you and they failed," he said. "The lion has claws. *Grrr!*"

The scout was from a Premiership club and Jimi's eyes sparkled when he came over to speak with him and Uncle Dani.

That evening he got his precious map of the world out for the first time in months. He found the club and drew a strip in the team's colours.

And, that night, Jimi dreamed of being part of a winning team, of moving around the pitch with power and pace, of perfect passes and shots on goal.

He woke up feeling that his dreams might come true at last.

AFRICA'S NATIONAL SIDES – NICKNAMES

Algeria – the Foxes

Cameroon – the Indomitable Lions

Congo – the Leopards

Gabon – the Panthers

Ivory Coast – the Elephants

Mali – the Eagles

Senegal – the Lions of Teranga

South Africa – Bafana, Bafana – "Go Boys, Go Boys"

Tunisia – the Eagles of Carthage

Chapter Six
The Lion Roars

Jimi was on the move again. He was going to a Premiership club.

"I'm flying to England," he told his family back home in Senegal. "Yes, they signed me."

Jimi saw his parents' smiling faces on the screen and he missed them. It was months since he'd been home to see them. Talking on Skype just wasn't the same as them being together.

"We are so proud of you," Dad said. "You worked hard at school, too. You didn't let your football take over."

Mum laughed. "Well, maybe a little. Uncle Dani says you are turning into a fine young man."

Jimi felt himself blush, and so he asked about his brother and sister.

"Nuru is studying for his exams. Julia has some exciting news too."

"I am going to Dakar to play in a tournament," Julia told him as her face came on the screen. "Maybe one day I'll play for the Senegal women's team. I'd like to be a coach and teach other girls how to play. There are plenty here who say we should stay in the kitchen, but ..." Julia stopped for a moment and looked Jimi straight in the eye. "Sometimes," she went on, "you have to break the rules to play the game."

Jimi was silent, thinking. He looked at his sister in awe. "Fantastic," he said at last. "I would love to go to one of your games. And maybe you will come here one day."

They talked for a long time. When they finished, Jimi was close to tears. He looked at the blank screen and wished some magic could bring his family closer to him, so he could give them great big hugs.

Jimi only saw them two or three times a year, but he wanted to see them all the time.

"I want them to be there when I play," he said.

Uncle Dani patted his arm. "Be patient," he told him. "If you work hard, you'll make enough money to fly them all over."

But when it was time for Jimi to fly to London, he was full of nerves – the thought of his new life did nothing but scare him. He felt dizzy at the thought of it.

"My English isn't as good as my French," he told Uncle Dani. "I don't know anyone in England."

"You're not a cub any more," Dani said, and he put his arm round him. "You're a lion. It's time to roar."

Jimi soon stopped being scared in England – there was no time to feel lonely either. He made friends with the other young players from France and Africa, and he spent the next year playing in the youth team and the reserves until one day he got the news. He was in the first team squad for an away match in London! He phoned Uncle Dani right away.

"I wish I could be there with you," his uncle said.

*

The day of the match, Jimi was so nervous he felt sick. For an hour he sat on the bench in the English cold, wondering if he would get a game. His team was 2–1 down with 15 minutes to go. Jimi looked at the manager as he made a substitution. He was hoping he would get a game, but the manager didn't choose him. Time was running out for Jimi. Then one of the team's star players went down under a strong tackle. He looked at the bench and shook his head. Jimi was on!

"Learn your lessons," he told himself as he finished his warm-up. "Be strong and play for the team."

With not long to go, the ball came Jimi's way. He tried to run with it, but he was too eager and lost it. It was another five minutes before he got it again. There were three minutes left on the clock and his team were still losing. This time he wasn't going to make the same mistake.

He controlled the ball and looked up. He could have overtaken the defender in front of him, but there was another man behind him. He saw a blur. It was his captain making a run into the box.

The defender lunged at Jimi, but he held the man off and rolled the ball towards his captain. The pass split the opposition defence and Jimi's captain swept it into the net. The crowd of away fans were on their feet.

2–2.

The captain ran towards Jimi. "You're the man," he shouted.

Jimi grinned until he thought his face would split. He had saved the match.

That's when a row of cheering faces caught his eye.

"No way," he said.

It was his whole family – Uncle Dani, Mum, Dad, Julia and Nuru. As soon as the referee blew for full time, he raced over to them.

"You're here!" he yelled. "How?"

"We have been saving," his mum said, her face wet with tears. "And Dani helped us too."

Jimi's eyes were stinging. "I will pay you back, Uncle Dani," he said as he tried to hug everyone all at the same time.

"Of course you will," Uncle Dani said. "Now you're the big star."

"We'll wait for you to get changed," Mum said as Jimi's team-mates left the field. "Go with the rest of your team."

As Jimi ran off to catch up with his team, the sound of the fans chanting his name over and over sent a shiver right through him.

"Jimi, Jimi Diop."

"Jimi, Jimi Diop!"

Jimi turned to wave to the crowd as he left the pitch and they answered him with a roar louder than anything he'd ever heard. The roar of the lion.

Our books are tested
for children and young people by
children and young people.

Thanks to everyone who consulted on
a manuscript for their time and effort in
helping us to make our books better
for our readers.